www.carameltree.com

The Legend of Rip Van Winkle

Chapter 1
Trouble

BANG!

Rip Van Winkle heard the gunshot and froze.

BANG! BANG! Two more gunshots and laughter.

Rip looked around in alarm.

These were dangerous times in Arizona. This was, after all, the place everyone called the Wild West.

Several more gunshots echoed across town. Rip dropped his bucket and dived into the cabbage patch. He knew better than to stay in view. Rip ducked down among the tall cabbage leaves and pulled his hat down. He heard horses galloping. He heard yells of "Yee-ha!"

It was the Clanton gang. The Clantons liked to ride into town shooting and shouting.

"Oh no!" Rip said. But there was no one listening. "What am I going to do?" Rip asked himself. But he had no answer. He was stuck. He would just have to wait until the Clantons left. And he would have to stay very quiet until then. Staying quiet was not difficult for Rip. He soon fell fast asleep!

"RIP VAN WINKLE!" shouted a voice. It was his mother, Mrs. Van Winkle. She was shouting from the kitchen. "You get here right now, Rip," she nagged. "Who's going to do all them chores?" Mrs. Van Winkle was angry.

Rip looked around sleepily. He was still worried about the Clantons, but they had gone. He had escaped. Now, all he had to do was to escape Mrs. Van Winkle's chores.

Chapter 2
Big and Strong

Rip crawled out of the cabbage patch so that Mrs. Van Winkle wouldn't see him. He was trying to escape all the chores she had for him. He crawled clear out of the yard.

"Escaped!" Rip said to himself. "Now I can go take a nap under the yucca tree," Rip sang.

Just as Rip was about to stand up, he
heard a voice.

"There's no escaping, young man!"

Rip froze! He was caught. But who could
it be? Rip was scared to even look up.

He didn't have to look too far up. It was a short man with blue eyes. He wore a star-shaped badge.

"You're the sheriff?" Rip gasped. "No one wants to be sheriff here! It's too dangerous! We have the… the…"

He was too frightened to say the name.

"Clantons?" the short man said. He smiled.

Rip shuddered.

"Well, I am Sheriff Wyatt Earp," said the short man. "And I'm here to bring law to this town."

Sheriff Earp shook Rip's hand. "I'm going to meet the Clantons. I want to take some people along – people like you, Rip. Let's show the Clantons we are serious."

Rip was shaking. "Me?" Rip looked down at the small sheriff.

"Yes! You!" Sheriff Earp grabbed Rip's arm.

"You are big and strong. You will scare those Clantons away," Sheriff Earp said.

Rip was not so sure. It's true that he was big and strong, but he was not very brave.

Rip looked sadly at the Sheriff. "I can't face the Clantons. I hide every time they come to town."

Sheriff Earp looked at Rip and smiled. "You might surprise yourself. Now let's go." The small sheriff walked on as Rip followed.

They soon reached the Town Square
where a group of people were waiting.

"Rip has agreed to join us," Sheriff Earp
announced. The little group cheered.

Rip looked at the group. Were these the
people that Sheriff Earp planned
to face the Clantons with? Rip
was sure that they were all
doomed.

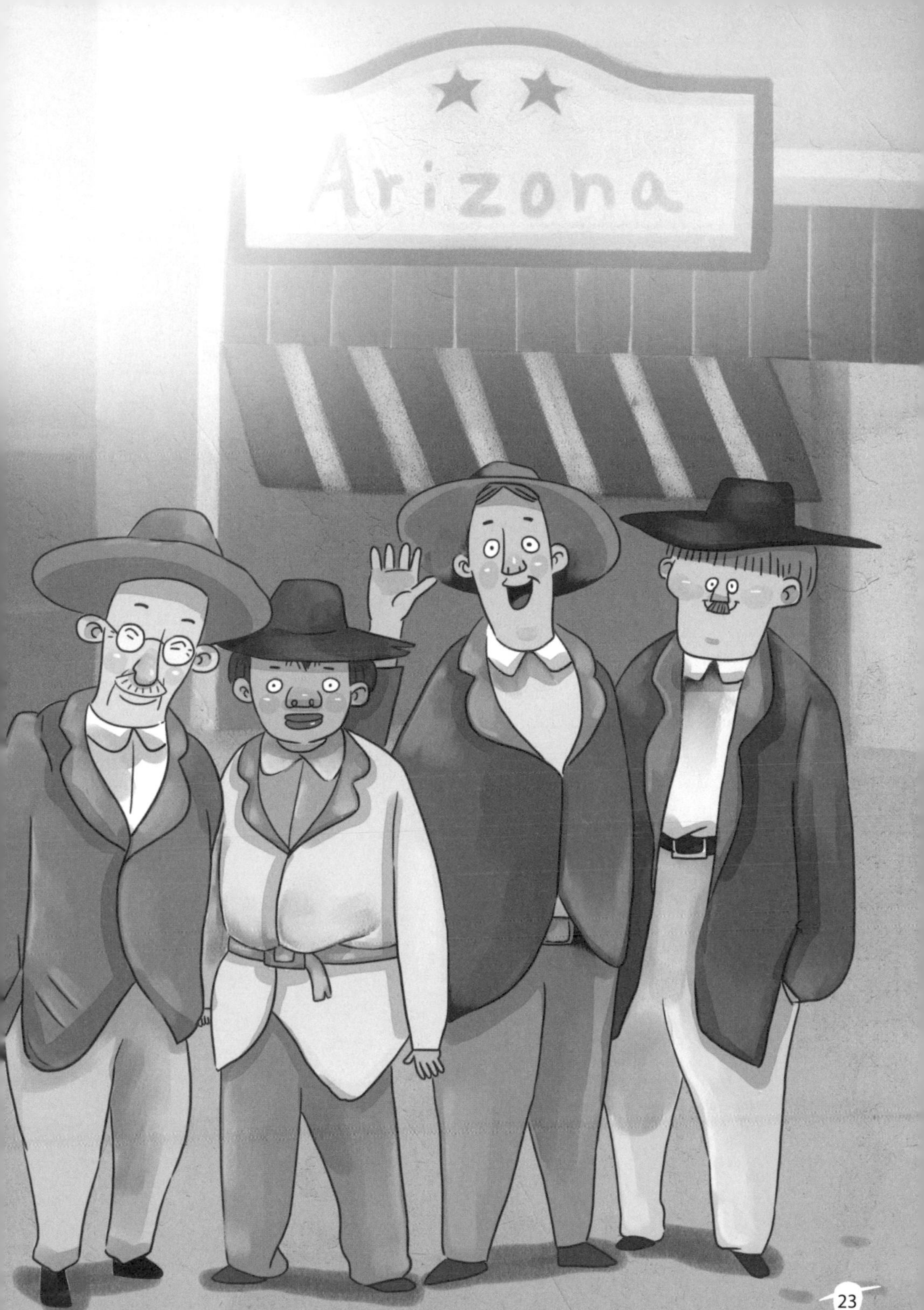
Arizona

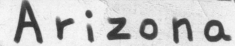

Rip, the other town folk and Sheriff Earp stood at one end of the street. The Clanton gang stood at the other end of the street.

One of the Clantons snarled, "Nobody stops us, Sheriff."

The Clantons drew their guns. They aimed at Sheriff Earp and his group.

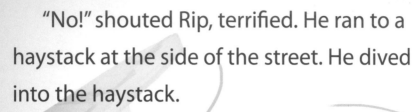

"No!" shouted Rip, terrified. He ran to a
haystack at the side of the street. He dived
into the haystack.

Behind him, he heard loud squeaks!
Then terrified yells, followed by gunshots.

Rip shut his eyes tightly...

Chapter 4
Napping Over

Prongs jabbed into Rip.

"All right, Mama," he mumbled. "I'll do them chores."

A voice – not his mother's – exclaimed, "A talking haystack?"

Rip opened his eyes. He wasn't napping under the yucca tree. He was in a haystack.

Now he remembered. Sheriff Earp had been facing down the Clantons. And then the Clantons had started shooting!

Rip scrambled out to the sidewalk.
"Please don't shoot!"

Wait. Sidewalk? The town had no
sidewalks.

Rip stared. The town was different. It was clean. It had shiny shops and restaurants. People in fancy clothes strolled by.

Nobody wore a gun.

Rip pulled hay out of his beard.

Beard? Rip had never had a beard. This one was down to his chest.

A man with a pitchfork frowned at him. "Get along, old-timer. I'm pulling down this haystack. We need to make a car park."

"A what?"

Beep, beep! A machine on four wheels slid past.

The driver spotted Rip. He braked.

"Rip Van Winkle?"

The driver was older than Rip remembered. But he still had kind blue eyes.

"Sheriff Earp?" gasped Rip.

Chapter 5
A Legend

"I'm not sheriff anymore. I retired twenty years ago," replied the old man.

Rip was confused. "Twenty years ago?"

"Sure enough," said the kind old man.

Rip froze. Had he been napping for twenty years? How could that be? What happened to the Clantons? Rip had many questions.

Wyatt Earp got out of his car and came over to Rip. "You are a legend!" he said, putting his arm around Rip.

"A legend?" Now Rip was very confused.

"It's 1911," Wyatt told Rip. "We were able to bring law and order to Arizona – because you helped chase the Clantons out twenty years ago."

"How?" asked Rip.

Wyatt said, "When you dived into the haystack, rats ran out, squeaking loudly. The rats startled the Clantons. They let out terrified yells. Instead of shooting at us, they aimed at the rats. But they missed!"

"The townspeople laughed at the Clantons. Bullies can't stand to be laughed at! The Clantons ran away. No one has heard of them since."

"You are a legend, Rip Van Winkle. Thanks to you, Arizona will become a state next year."

Rip gulped. "A state? Part of a real country?"

"Yep!" Wyatt smiled.

Rip smiled, too. Then he thought of something. "How is my mother?"

Wyatt grinned. "She's at home, Rip. She's been waiting for you."

Rip thought of something else that would be waiting for him. Twenty years' worth of chores!